My name is _____ and I am

_____ years of age. This book has been

given to me by _____ who is getting

married to _____ . I have been asked

to be a Bridesmaid at their Wedding which will

take place at _____ on

_____ . I know the Bride and

Groom because _____ .

This edition published in 1998

Published by Blitz Editions, an imprint of Bookmart Limited
Registered Number 2372865
Trading as Bookmart Limited
Desford Road, Enderby, Leicester, LE9 5AD

Copyright © Text Caroline Plaisted 1996
Copyright © Illustrations Joanna Walsh 1996
Designed by Lisa Coombes
The moral right of the author and illustrator has been asserted

ISBN 1 85605 406 3

Printed in Hong Kong by C&C Offset Co., Ltd
10 9 8 7 6 5 4 3 2 1

My Day As A Bridesmaid

Caroline Plaisted

Illustrated by
Joanna Walsh

BLITZ EDITIONS

Congratulations

Congratulations! You have been chosen to be one of the special people on a very important occasion. Being a Bridesmaid will be exciting but you will have lots of jobs to do on the Wedding Day and a great deal to remember.

This book will help you to prepare for the day in advance. It tells you who all the special people will be at the Wedding. There are details of all the things you will be expected to do and what you should practise so that you are perfect on the day. There are even special sections for you to record the important details and a special place to keep photographs and mementos.

You will always remember your day as a Bridesmaid.

Who Will be at the Wedding

Some Brides like to have only a few guests at their Wedding, whilst others might invite lots of people. However big or small the Wedding is, the following people will definitely be there:

The Bride and Groom

The two most important people! Without them you wouldn't have been asked to be a Bridesmaid.

The Celebrant

In a Church this will be a Priest who might be referred to as the Vicar or Minister. In a Synagogue, there will be a Rabbi. At a Register Office, the celebrant will be a Registrar.

The Best Man

He'll probably be the best friend or a close relative of the Groom. He's there to help the Groom and to make sure that everything goes smoothly. At the Service he looks after the Wedding rings. At the Reception he will read out any special messages for the Bride and Groom and make a speech.

At a lot of Weddings, you'll also find these people:

The Chief Bride or Matron of Honour

She'll look after the Bride all day and will probably look after all the Bride's attendants.

The Bridesmaids

Other girls like you. Bridesmaids can be very young or can be grown ups.

The Pageboys

Little boys who will also follow the Bride on her Wedding Day.

The Ushers

These are usually men and their job is to help the Best Man. Most importantly, they show the Wedding guests to their seats at the Wedding Ceremony.

The Bridesmaids' Duties

Bridesmaids are chosen to attend the Bride on her Wedding Day – they are the "Maids" of the Bride or her attendants. Some Brides have only one Bridesmaid but others have a small group and perhaps some Pageboys as well.

You musn't worry about not knowing what you will be expected to do on the Wedding Day because someone will make sure that you do. If there is a Chief Bridesmaid or Matron of Honour, she will look after you and the Bride as well. And you will probably have a rehearsal together with the Bride and Groom, as well as those other people with an important part to play on the day.

The Wedding Day is a long, busy day. This will give you an idea of what to expect:

In the Morning

You will probably be asked to arrive at the Bride's home early in the morning so that you can get dressed and have your hair done. Sometimes, photographs are taken of everyone getting ready and looking pretty in their dresses before they leave for the service. It will be the Chief Bridesmaid or Matron of Honour who helps the Bride to get ready.

The Journey

The Wedding Ceremony may be held in a Church, Register Office, a Synagogue or another special place. Usually there will be a short journey from the Bride's home to the venue. You may be asked to make the journey in a car or perhaps in a horse-drawn coach or another special type of transport. You will travel with all the other Bridesmaids and Pageboys and will be expected to arrive at least ten minutes before the Bride. When you get there, you may have some more photographs taken while you wait for the Bride.

During the Service

Once the Bride arrives, the Bridesmaids should help to make sure that the Bride's dress isn't crumpled. It is the Chief Bridesmaid's job to check the Bride's veil and train.

All the Bridesmaids and Pageboys then take their places and follow the Bride and her father down the aisle towards the Groom. The Chief Bridesmaid then takes the Bride's flowers and looks after them during the Service.

In a Church, the ceremony is taken by a Priest who stands facing the Bride and Groom at the Chancel steps. In a Synagogue the couple are married by a Rabbi under a *chuppah* or wedding canopy. In a Register Office, the couple are married standing before the Registrar.

The Bridesmaids usually remain standing for most of the Ceremony although you will probably be asked to sit at certain times. After the Register has been signed, the Bridesmaids and Pageboys follow the Bride and Groom as they leave the Ceremony. If one of the Bridesmaids is a Flower Girl, she will walk in front of the Bride and Groom and scatter flower petals or confetti in their path.

More photographs will then be taken before the couple are sprinkled with confetti and after that they leave for the reception.

The Reception

After another short car journey, the
Bridesmaids arrive at the reception, just
after the Bride and Groom. You may be
asked to take part in a Receiving Line
(this is the Bride's and Groom's chance
to greet all of the guests formally).
Sometimes people sit down to eat a meal,
sometimes there is a buffet instead. At the
end of the meal, there will be speeches given by
the Bride's father, the Best Man and the Groom, who has the job
of toasting the Bridesmaids to thank them for doing their job so
well. The Wedding Cake is then cut and given to the guests.

At some Weddings, there will then be some dancing before the
Bride and Groom leave.

The Going Away

All the guests will want to see the Bride and
Groom leave in style so everyone will cheer and
they may throw more confetti over them. Just
before they go, the Bride will throw her bouquet
to her guests. It is said that the lady who catches
it will be the next person to get married!

Write down here how excited
you are about being asked to
be a Bridesmaid:

_____

_____

_____

_____

_____

These are the things that I am
nervous about:

_____

_____

_____

_____

_____

Things to Practise

There will be a long time during the Service and the Reception when you have to be quiet and patient so it would be a good idea to practise how to sit still for as long as possible. Perhaps you could ask someone to time you doing this? You could keep a record of how long you manage each time you try. As you will be having lots of photographs taken you could practise smiling a lot and saying "Cheese" whilst you look in the mirror. (Saying this makes you look like you are smiling.) Make sure you are good at walking slowly up and down the aisle. A good place to do this would be a hallway or corridor.

Photo/Drawing Section

On their Wedding Day, the Bride and Groom will be wearing special clothes and will look quite different from usual. Why not take a photograph of them, or draw their picture, of what they look like on a normal day in their ordinary clothes?

Clothes and Shoes

One of the loveliest things about being a Bridesmaid is that you will be given a pretty dress and special shoes to wear. Your dress might be made of silk, velvet, or cotton, and it will probably be in one of the Bride's favourite colours. You might have an identical dress to the other Bridesmaids or it is possible that each of you will wear a different colour. If there is a Chief Bridesmaid, or Matron of Honour, her dress will probably be a different style. For instance, her dress might be long and yours might be shorter – but they could be the same colour.

You might be asked to go to a dressmaker to have your measurements taken and fittings for your dress. Perhaps you will know the

dressmaker, as she might be a relative of yours or the Bride's. Alternatively, you might go on a special shopping trip with the Bride to buy a dress from a shop. There are special shops that sell only dresses for Brides and Bridesmaids. Wherever your dress comes from, it is important to tell the dressmaker or the shop assistant if your dress or shoes are too tight or uncomfortable.

Whatever kind of dress you have, you will almost certainly have to go on a special shopping trip to buy some shoes. You might be bought shiny satin ballet shoes which will be dyed to match your dress, or perhaps you will be given some patent leather shoes or some sandals to wear.

My dress is being made out of:

_____

The colour of my dress is:

_____

My dress is being made by:

_____

My first fitting is on:

_____

My final fitting is on:

_____

My dress was bought from:

_____

The colour of my shoes is:

_____

My shoes are made out of:

_____

My shoes were bought from:

_____

Things to Practise

Walking along in a pair of jeans and trainers
is quite different from walking behind the
Bride and wearing a special dress and
shoes. Your dress will probably be longer
and have a fuller skirt than the ones you have
worn before. It would be a good idea to practise walking in your
dress a couple of times before the Wedding. If you have the
dress at home, always check with your mother before
you try it on. Imagine if you ripped your dress or
accidently spilt something on it! If you can't
practise walking in your own dress, why
don't you ask your mother if you can
borrow a dress that someone else
wore to be a Bridesmaid, or
perhaps a party frock you
could practise in?

It is important to make sure that you can walk without slipping in your new shoes but don't forget to ask someone if you can try on the shoes before you practise. You don't want your shoes to look dirty and worn out by the Wedding Day, do you? If the soles of your shoes are slippery, ask a grown up if they can do something to them to make sure you don't fall over. And don't forget to take the price ticket off the soles as well!

Because you will be going in a car in your smart new clothes and shoes, practise sitting down and standing up without creasing your dress. The place where the ceremony is to take place might have steps leading to the door so you will also want to try going up and down the stairs without catching your shoes in your hem. (It doesn't matter if you do fall over but you would probably prefer not to!) Finally, if you can, find a suitable place for a hankie – you don't want to have to wipe your nose on your pretty sleeves! If there isn't anywhere, ask your mother if she can keep a handkerchief handy for you.

Photo/Drawing Section

Draw a picture of your pretty dress and shoes here. You could also ask someone to take a photograph of you whilst you are having a fitting for your dress and you could keep that here as well.

Hair

You will probably be asked to go to a hairdresser to find out what sort of hair style you will have on the Wedding Day. Sometimes the hairdresser visits you at the Bride's home. The style that is chosen will depend on the length of your hair and the type of headdress that you will wear. The hairdresser will want to practise doing your hair so that she can make sure your headdress stays securely in place without your hair falling in your eyes. (To do this, she might put some hairspray on it.) The headdress might be like a hat or it could be similar to a headband. Or perhaps the Bride has chosen for you to wear a garland of flowers in your hair. These may be real flowers which match the posy of flowers that you are to carry, or might be made of paper or silk to match your dress.

On the Wedding Day, the hairdresser usually visits the Bride's house and makes sure that everyone's hair is done properly so that it will stay in place for the whole day.

The hairdresser's name is:

_____

I went to the hairdresser for the first time on:

_____

The colour of my headdress is:

_____

My headdress will look like:

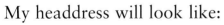

_____

_____

Things to Practise

On the day of the Wedding you will be expected to have neat and tidy hair all day. So you need to practise not bumping into things and knocking your hair. Ask if you can practise wearing your headdress by spending a couple of hours with it in your hair so that you get used to it. (Don't play any rough games

though because you don't want to spoil your headdress before the Wedding Day!) Make sure that you rehearse walking with your head up. If you walk along looking at the ground, the Wedding guests won't be able to see your face and any photographs will show only the top of your head! Practise getting in and out of the car as well. You'll need to tuck your head down as you do, so that you don't catch your headdress on the doorframe. And if you have a long dress, don't forget to lift it carefully, as if you are going to curtsey, so you don't stand on it!

Photo/Drawing Section

You could ask someone to take a photograph of you once the hairdresser has finished, or you could draw a picture of your headdress here:

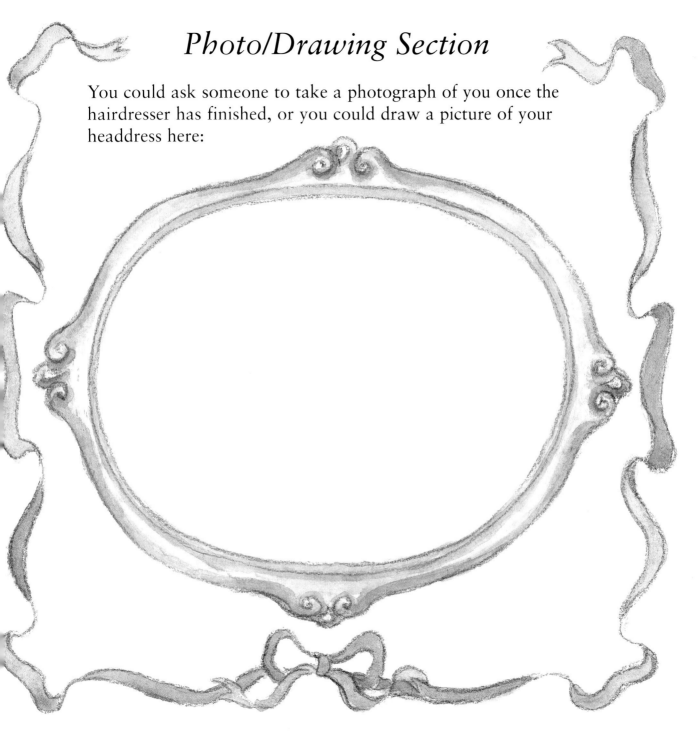

The Other Bridesmaids and Pageboys

It might be that you already know all or some of the other Bride's attendants. They could be your sisters or cousins, or perhaps they are friends or Godchildren of the Bride and Groom. Sometimes the Bride will have Pageboys as well. If there are going to be lots of you, the Bride might have a Matron of Honour or Chief Bridesmaid. She is usually older than the other Bridesmaids and will probably look after you and all the other Bride's attendants on the Wedding Day. The youngest little girl might be a Flower Girl. She will be asked to scatter petals in the Bride's path as she leaves the ceremony.

A short while before the Wedding, the Bride will arrange for you to meet the other Bridesmaids and Pageboys. This might be when you have the first fitting for your special clothes or perhaps there might be a tea party arranged so that you can all get to know each other. (Don't forget to make a note of who they all are in the record section.)

The Names of the other Bridesmaids are:

1 _____

She knows the Bride and

Groom because:_____

_____

2 _____

She knows the Bride and

Groom because:_____

_____

3 _____

She knows the Bride and

Groom because:_____

_____

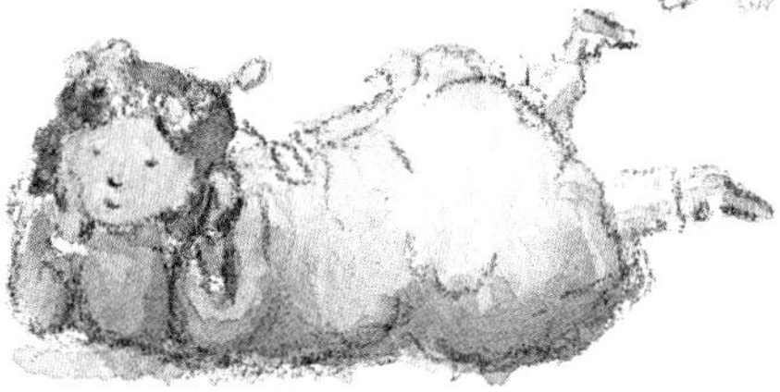

4 _____

She knows the Bride and

Groom because:_____

_____

5 _____

She knows the Bride and

Groom because:_____

_____

6 _____

She knows the Bride and

Groom because:_____

_____

The Names of the Pageboys are:

1 _____

He knows the Bride and

Groom because:_____

_____

2 _____

He knows the Bride and

Groom because:_____

_____

3 _____

He knows the Bride and

Groom because:_____

_____

4 _____

He knows the Bride and

Groom because:_____

_____

5 _____

He knows the Bride and

Groom because:_____

_____

6 _____

He knows the Bride and

Groom because:_____

_____

Things to Practise

It is very important that you get on well with all the other Bridesmaids and Pageboys so if you don't already know them try hard to be friends. On the Wedding Day you may be asked to hold hands with one of the others as you walk behind the Bride before and after the Wedding ceremony. One of the reasons the Bride will have asked you to be a Bridesmaid is because she knows that you are going to be very good at this.

Even so, it would be a good idea to practise walking up and
down with the others. Make sure that you don't trip over each
other and that you remember to hold your heads up and look in
front of you! Ask one of the grown ups if they know which
order you will walking in and then you can have an early
rehearsal in the right places.

Photo/Drawing Section

Ask someone if they can take a photograph of you with all the others when you first get together. Or perhaps you would prefer to draw your own picture of what everyone looks like.

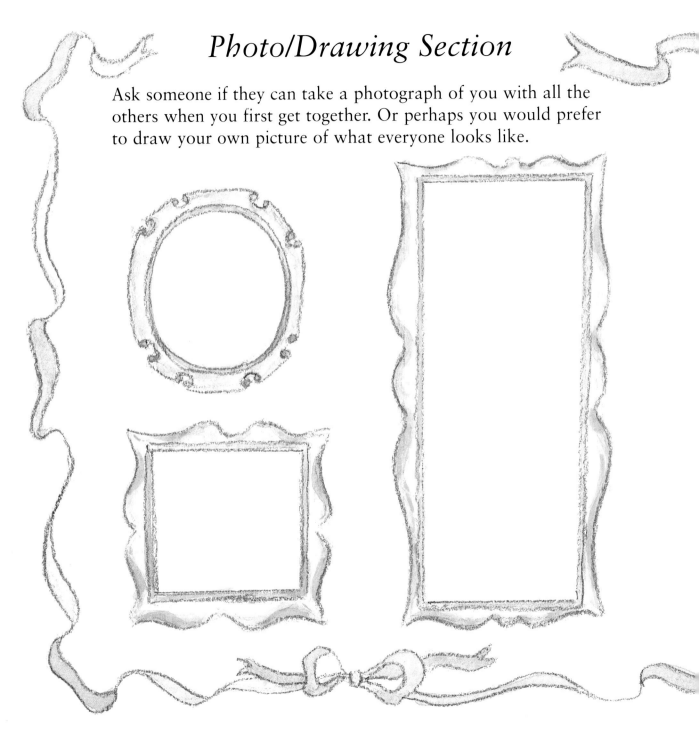

The Rehearsal

Because a Wedding is so important, a rehearsal will almost certainly be held. This is usually on the day before the Wedding itself and, if you haven't met everyone before, you will get the chance to meet them now. The rehearsal will be attended by the Bride and Groom, all the Bridesmaids and Page Boys, the Best Man, the Bride's parents and perhaps the Groom's parents, and the person who will be taking the Service. The reason for the rehearsal is for everyone to learn exactly what they are to do at the Wedding and where they should walk and stand. Remember, someone will make sure that you know exactly what to do and when. So don't get nervous about it.

The rehearsal was held on:

_____

_____

It was taken by:

_____

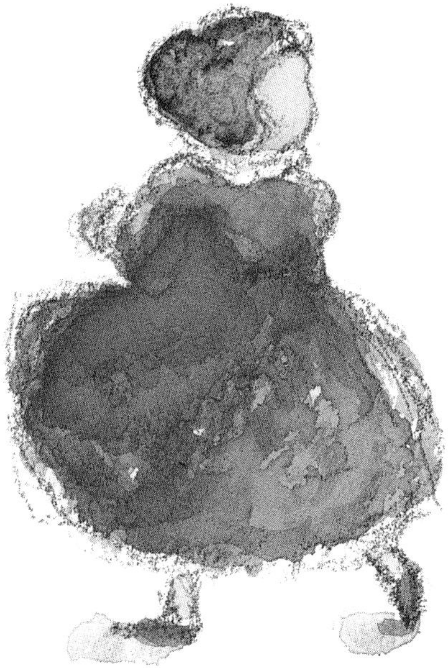

_____ It took place at:

_____

_____

The people at the rehearsal were:

_____

_____

Things to Practise

If you've practised everything else so far, you will be an expert at the rehearsal. Make sure that you learn where to stand and walk – if you aren't certain, check things with the Chief Bridesmaid, Matron of Honour, or the Bride's mother. Practise walking with your head up and looking in front of you, trying to walk at the same speed as everyone else. (This is especially important if the Bride is wearing a long train as part of her outfit, as you don't want to tread on it and rip it!)

Try to rehearse holding your posy of flowers so that you don't hold them so high no one can see your face or that you don't hold them out at the side and bash someone with them!

And don't forget that you will want to smile as much as possible throughout the day so practise your smile as well!

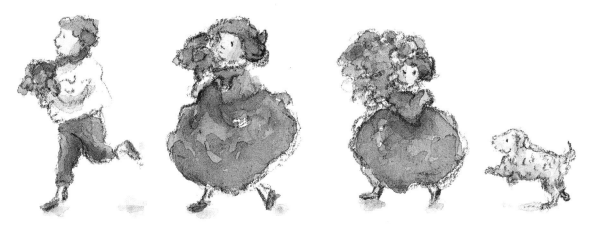

Photo/Drawing Section

Someone might take photographs of the rehearsal so you might want to ask them to let you have a photograph to put here. Just like you, the Bride will also be wearing casual clothes rather than her beautiful dress although she might also be wearing her train or veil for everyone to practise with at the rehearsal. Why not draw a picture of her with the Groom showing how they looked?

The Wedding Day

It's arrived at last. Like everyone else involved with the Wedding you'll be very excited. So here is a countdown of everything so that you don't forget anything.

Breakfast

Make sure you have something to eat at the start of the day. If you have, you will be less likely to suffer from a "butterfly tummy" and your stomach won't rumble loudly during the quiet moments of the Service.

A Bath

You don't want to be grubby and smelly, so have a bath or shower just after you get up in the morning. Check with the hairdresser to see if you should wash your hair as well or whether they will want to do this. It is important that you bathe before the hairdresser does your hair so that you don't damage your pretty hairstyle and headdress!

46

Your Hair

Even though you will be excited and impatient to get to the Wedding, try your best to sit still whilst you have your hair done and the headdress is put on. If you have to visit the hairdresser to have your hair done, don't forget to take an umbrella with you to protect your hair if it is raining as you walk from the salon to the car.

Getting Dressed

Make sure you go to the loo before you get dressed! Put your tights or socks on first because it will be difficult to get them on once you are wearing everything else. Remember to ask for help to step into your dress and then pull it up to your shoulders. (If you pull your dress over your head you will damage your hairstyle and headdress.) Put your shoes on last.

47

The Journey to the Service

You will probably be given your flowers just before you set off – don't forget to take them with you! If you suffer from travel sickness, ask your mother to give you something to help you before you leave. You will travel with either the Chief Bridesmaid or the Bride's mother so, if you don't feel well, ask them to open the car window straight away.

The Service

Before you go in, check that your dress isn't crumpled. If you need to blow your nose, do it now. Wait quietly for the Bride to arrive and don't forget to smile and say hello to her when she does. It would be nice if you told her how lovely she looked too. Try not to fidget during the service, and join in with the hymns if you know them.

The Photographs

These might take a very long time but it should be fun. The photographer will tell you what to do and when to do it. Don't forget to smile and keep your hands and feet straight because otherwise they'll look funny in the photographs!

The Reception

You'll probably need to go to the loo again as
soon as you get there. (You might need help
because of your special dress so don't be
embarassed to ask for it.) Make sure that your
dress isn't tucked into your knickers before you
wash your hands and face and go back into the Reception.

Every Reception is different. Some are formal and everyone sits
down to eat. Others are informal and might have a buffet where
you go and help yourself to food, or there might be waiters and
waitresses who bring the food and wine around the room to
the guests. If you are sitting down to eat, someone will tell you

where to go. As part of the Bridal party, you will probably be seated at the most important place, which is called the Top Table. Make sure that you talk to the guests sitting next to you during the meal. At some stage, the Wedding Cake will be cut by the Bride and Groom.

Sit quietly during the speeches – and don't forget to pay special attention when the Groom makes a toast to thank you and the other Bridesmaids. The Best Man will reply on your behalf to say how happy you were to be such an important part of this special day.

The Going Away

When the Bride and Groom leave the Reception it is called Going Away because they are usually off on their Honeymoon. Everyone likes to cheer when they leave and wish them well. Sometimes people throw confetti now – make sure you've got some to sprinkle them with too. Just before she leaves, the Bride usually turns her back on her guests and tosses her bouquet over her head towards them. See if you can catch it! Turn back to page 15 if you can't remember why. (Don't forget to take some Wedding Cake home with you. Wrap a tiny piece in a paper napkin and place it under your pillow before you go to sleep. To find out why, turn to page 61.)

There were _____ people at the Wedding and their names were:

_____   _____   _____

_____   _____   _____

_____   _____   _____

_____   _____

_____   _____

_____   _____

_____   _____

_____   _____

_____   _____

_____   _____   _____

_____   _____   _____

_____   _____   _____

The weather was:

_____

I thought that the Wedding
Service was:

_____

The Reception was held at:

_____

This is what we had to eat
and drink:

_____

_____

_____

_____

Their Honeymoon will be
spent in:

_____

The Bride's bouquet was:

_____

The Bride and Groom left the
Reception at:

_____

I went to bed at:

_____

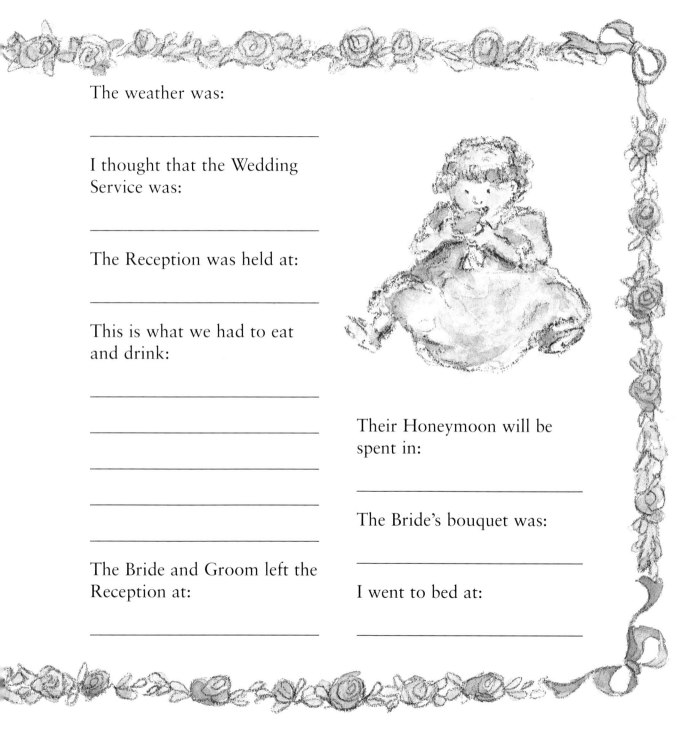

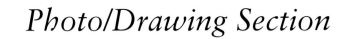

Photo/Drawing Section

Why not dry some of your flowers and keep them here? (To do this, press them between some sheets of blotting paper inside a heavy book.) You could make a special picture of them and decorate it with some of the confetti which you have saved. When the photographs are developed you will probably be sent one, so you could keep it in here to remind you of how special you all looked at the Wedding.

(There is a special envelope at the front of this book where you can keep your Wedding souvenirs such as an Invitation, the Order of Service and any other special Wedding things.)

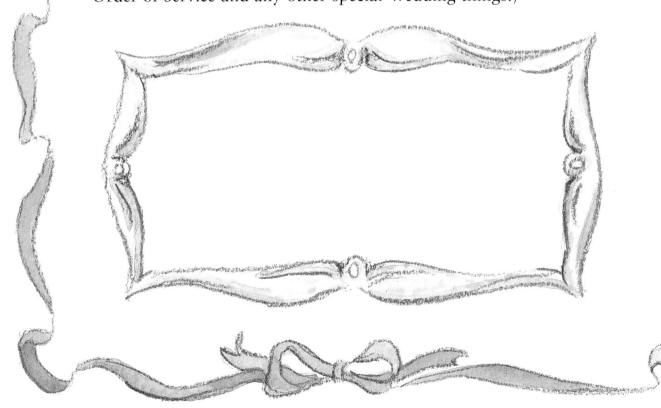

The Day After The Wedding

After the Wedding you might be feeling a bit sad that all the excitement is over and that you can't wear your special dress until you next go to a party. Why not finish writing in your records and memories of the day? Remembering all the happy things will cheer you up.

It would be nice to write to the Bride and her mother to thank them for such a special day. If the Groom gave you a present to thank you for being a Bridesmaid, you should also write to him.

If you can't think what to write, here are some suggestions:

To the Bride

Dear   , Thank you for asking me to be a bridesmaid at your wedding. I had a lovely time and felt very special in my pretty clothes. I thought that you looked beautiful.

With love from,

To the Groom

Dear   , Thank you for your special gift which I will always treasure. I thought you made a handsome groom and I really enjoyed my day as a bridesmaid.

With love from,

To the Bride's Mother

Dear   , Thank you for the lovely wedding reception. I really enjoyed it and thought the food was scrumptious. The bride looked beautiful.

With love from,

The Wedding Cake

There is a legend which says that if you go to bed with a piece of Wedding Cake under your pillow, you will have sweet dreams of the man you are going to marry! Did you remember to save some cake? If you did, who was the man of your dreams?

The things I liked best about being a
Bridesmaid were:

_____

_____

_____

_____

_____

_____